LIBRARY OF DOOM

THE EYE IN THE GRAVEYARD

by Michael Dahl
Illustrated by Fernando Molinari

STONE ARCH BOOKS
a capstone imprint

Library of Doom is published by Stone Arch Books,
A Capstone imprint
1710 Roe Crest Drive
North Mankato, Minnesota 56003
www.mycapstone.com

Library of Congress Cataloging-in-Publication Data
is available on the Library of Congress website.

ISBN: 978-1-4965-5528-1 (library binding)
ISBN: 978-1-4965-5534-2 (paperback)
ISBN: 978-1-4965-5540-3 (eBook PDF)

Summary: The Librarian delivers an evil book to a
tall tower in a mysterious graveyard.

Designer: Brent Slingsby

Photo credits:
Design Element: Shutterstock: Shebeko.

Printed and bound in the USA.
112017 010943R

Table of Contents

Quickly, the Librarian races up the stairs.

He can feel the tower sinking beneath his feet.

If he doesn't reach the door soon, he will be buried alive . . .

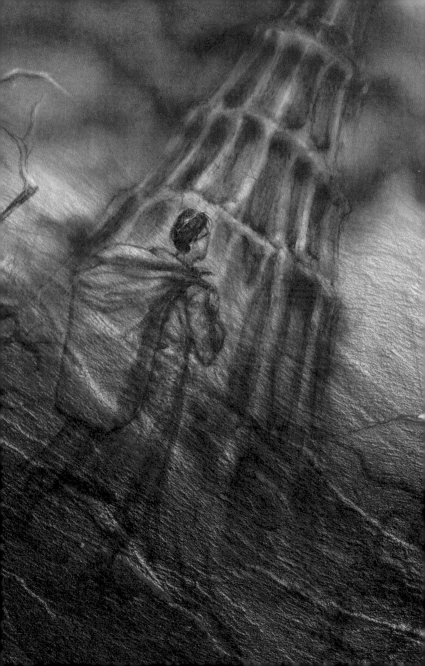

THE LIBRARIAN

Real name: unknown
Parents: unknown
Birthplace/birthdate: unknown
Weaknesses: water, crumbs, dirty fingers
Strengths: speed reading, ability to fly, martial arts

THE LIBRARY

The Library of Doom is the world's largest collection of strange and dangerous books. Each generation, a new Librarian is chosen to serve as guardian. The Librarian's duty is to keep the books from falling into the hands of those who would use them for evil.

The location of the Library of Doom is unknown. Its shelves sit partially hidden underground. Some sections form a maze. It is full of black holes. This means someone might walk down a hallway in the Library and not realize they are traveling thousands of miles. One hallway could start somewhere under the Atlantic Ocean and end inside the caves of the Himalayas.

There are entries to the Library scattered all over the earth. But there are few exits. Sometimes villains find their way into the vast collection, but the Librarian always finds them out!

— From *The Atlas Cryptical*, compiled by Orson Drood, 5th official Librarian

CHAPTER ONE

THE HEAVY BAG

Ghostly moonlight shines on a vast **graveyard**.

A thin shadow moves through the graveyard, bending the grass.

It is the Librarian. He drags a heavy bag behind him.

A dark bird sits on a gravestone. Its eyes shine like drops of **ink**. Carefully, it watches the Librarian pass.

The Librarian wipes the sweat from his forehead. Tired, he leans against a tall gravestone.

He looks down at the name carved into the stone. He reads `Here Lies the First Librarian`.

The Librarian bends down and then grabs the bag again.

Inside the bag is something heavier than anything he has carried before.

It is an evil book.

He has brought the book here to bury it.

CHAPTER TWO

THE GLASS EYE

The Librarian looks across the **graveyard**.

He sees five dark shapes above the grass.

At the top of the tallest shape is a `bright`, round eye.

The Librarian has heard stories about the Eye of the Graveyard.

From one of the stories, the Librarian remembers strange words:

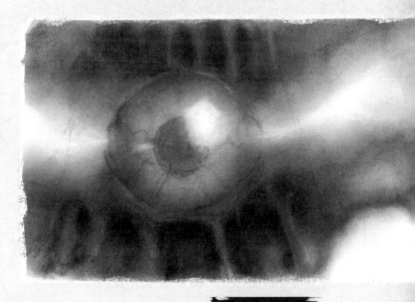

"To escape the darkness
A man must lose his eye."

The Librarian's bag grows
heavier. It falls to the ground.

A cloud passes in front of the
moon. The bright eye grows dim
and disappears.

Behind him, the Librarian
can hear the black bird croaking.

The Librarian moves closer
to the tall, **black shapes.**

The cloud drifts away from
the moon.

The eye opens again. It **gleams**
like silver.

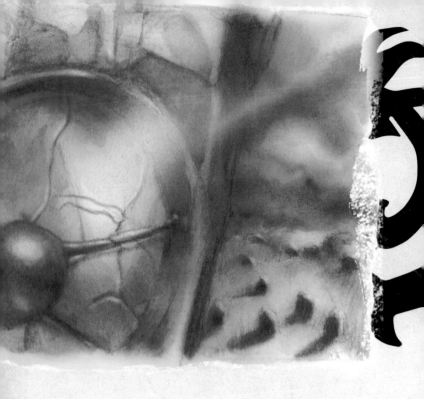

The Librarian laughs to himself.
The eye is really a glass window in a
high tower.

CHAPTER THREE

INTO THE TOWER

The Librarian stops smiling.
This tower is the one he has been
looking for. The evil book will
be buried inside the tallest of the
five towers.

The book grows **heavier**
inside the bag.

The Librarian can barely
drag it through the door in the
tower's side.

Steep, curving stairs lead down.
At each step, the book inside the
bag hits against the stone.

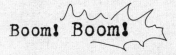

Boom! Boom!

Echoes shake the shadows.

The Librarian reaches the last
step at the bottom of the tower.
He is dripping with sweat.

He drops the bag and looks
around him.

He is standing at the entrance
to a gigantic tomb. A **tomb** for books.

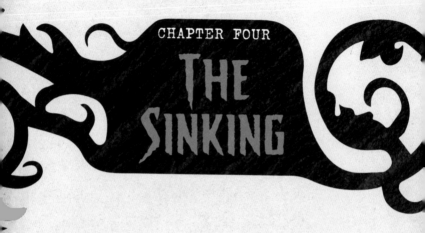

CHAPTER FOUR

THE SINKING

The Librarian takes two gloves
from his belt and puts them on.
Then he pulls the dangerous book
from its bag.

In the center of the tomb is a stone
table. The Librarian sets the book on
the table and chains it into place.

The Librarian stares at the evil pages. He takes a deep breath. The book can never leave this place.

It will never **harm** anyone again.

Then the table shakes.
The tomb shudders.

The book is **shaking.**

It breaks its chains and snaps the locks. The stone table is **crushed** beneath the book's great weight.

Then the **tomb shivers** again.

The graveyard tower is sinking!

The evil book is pushing it deep into the ground.

Quickly, the Librarian races up the stairs. He can feel the tower sinking beneath his feet.

If he doesn't reach the door soon, he will be buried alive inside the tower.

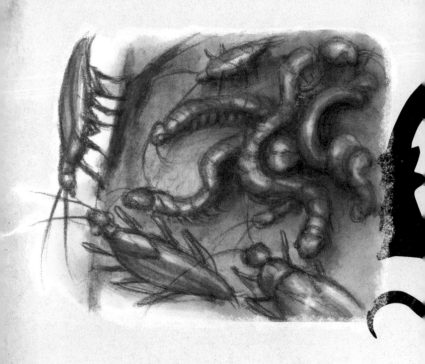

He reaches the top of the stairs,
but he is too late. The doorway has
sunk below the ground.

Worms and bugs fill the space.

He is **trapped** inside.

CHAPTER FIVE
LOSING THE EVE

The Librarian hears a croak.
He looks up and sees a bird's shadow
on the wall high above him.

Where does the **shadow**
come from?

The Librarian remembers
the window, the glass eye. He
remembers the words of the story.

"To escape the darkness
A man must lose his eye."

The Librarian runs up the
stairs of the tower as it sinks
into the graveyard.

He reaches the top.

He covers his face with his
arms. He throws himself **against
the window.**

It shatters into a thousand pieces.

The eye is lost.

The Librarian has escaped the **darkness.**

With a horrible rumble, all
five towers sink into the ground.

Weary and wounded, the
Librarian lies nearby. He turns
over on his back to face the sky.

A breeze blows through the graveyard. The black sky begins to turn blue.

Somewhere, a bird begins to sing.

~ THE END ~

NOTES FROM THE LIBRARIAN

Some books are dangerous without ever being opened. Beware anything written by the outlaw author, Nocturna Tome. She places curses on the covers of her books. If a reader simply says the title out loud, something terrible will happen. If the reader rubs their hand along the book's spine — it's too late. I have seen Tome's victims turn to stone, shoot up into space, or disappear in sudden storms of falling frogs.

Tome wrote the book in this adventure. I can't tell you the title, but it was an atlas that showed all the evil places on the planet. I couldn't afford to have anyone open the book, touch it, or read its words aloud. It was too dangerous even for the Library of Doom. Now the book lies buried in the graveyard in the sunken tower beneath the earth. There are no marks showing where the tower once stood. The secret of its resting spot will die with me.

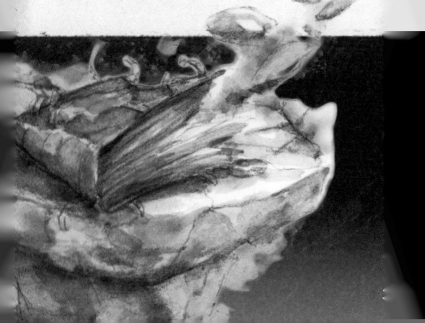

A Page from the Library of Doom

Epitaphs

Epitaphs (EP-uh-tafs) are the words found on a gravestone or memorial that tell something about the person buried there. Here are a few.

Underneath this stone
Lies poor John Round,
Lost at sea and never found.

First a cough
Carried me off,
Then a coffin
They carried me off in.

Here lies what's left
Of Lester Moore,
No Les
No more.

Here lies Pecos Bill,
He always lied
And always will,
He once lied loud,
He now lies still.

About the Author

Michael Dahl is the prolific author of the bestselling *Goodnight Baseball* picture book and more than two hundred other books for children and young adults. He has won the AEP Distinguished Achievement Award three times for his nonfiction, a Teachers' Choice Award from *Learning* magazine, and a Seal of Excellence from the Creative Child Awards. Dahl currently lives in Minneapolis, Minnesota.

About the Illustrator

Fernando Molinari was born in Argentina and has worked as an illustrator and art instructor. He has illustrated magazines, CD covers, comics, graphic novels, and books (including Anne Rice's *Lasher*). His artwork has been shown in various galleries and museums throughout the United States, as well as in The Museum of Modern Art in Buenos Aires. Molinari has won numerous awards and has also appeared on TV to discuss his art and demonstrate his techniques.

Glossary

croak (KROHK)—a deep, scratchy cry or call

gleam (GLEEM)—to shine

rumble (RUM-buhl)—a low noise that sounds like thunder

shatter (SHAT-ur)—to break into lots of smaller pieces

shudder (SHUD-ur)—to shake quickly with fear

vast (VAST)—very big or gigantic

DISCUSSION QUESTIONS

1. Why do you think the Librarian drags the book inside a bag instead of carrying it by hand?

2. The graveyard is a creepy place, but is it dangerous? Why or why not? Is there anything in the story that gives you a clue that the Librarian might get into trouble in the graveyard?

3. When the Librarian is trapped in the tower, he looks up and sees the shadow of the bird. The shadow reminds him of the window. Do you think the bird was trying to help the Librarian on purpose? Why or why not?

WRITING PROMPTS

1. The book inside the bag is evil, but we
    don't know how it is evil. What makes
    the book so dangerous? What happens
    to people when they read it? Write your
    own ideas about the heavy book.

2. What would have happened if the
    Librarian never jumped out the window?
    Would he be trapped forever? Or would
    he have found another way to escape?

3. Read the epitaphs on the facts pages
    (pages 38 and 39). Then write your own
    epitaph for an imaginary person who
    has died. It can be funny, serious, or
    even scary.

BUILDING THE LIBRARY

Some words from author Michael Dahl

When I lived in Charleston, South Carolina, I visited a haunted neighborhood in the heart of the old city. The 180-year-old St. Philip's Church covered almost an entire block. A ghostly priest was often seen on the front steps at night. Some evenings he climbed the tower and rang one of the bells. Across the street in a graveyard, the girlfriend of Edgar Allen Poe lies buried. People have seen a dark shadowy figure gliding among the gravestones.

I had been performing in a theater a few blocks from the church. After the shows, I had to walk past the graveyard on my way to the parking lot. Breezes stirred the hanging moss on the trees. Tall grass shivered between the tombstones. One night I saw a stooping, shadowy figure. Was it Poe visiting his girlfriend? That eerie graveyard and the haunted church tower crept into my brain, sank into my imagination, and eventually grew into the setting for this adventure.

EXPLORE THE ENTIRE
LIBRARY OF DOOM

THE DIGITAL ARCHIVES

DISCOVER MORE AT:

capstonekids.com

Authors and Illustrators
Videos and Contests
Games and Puzzles
Heroes and Villains

Find cool websites and
more books like this one
at www.facthound.com

Just type in the Book ID:
9781496555281
and you're ready to go!